"For Robert Bernheim— teacher, scholar and
professor— who taught me monsters are real,
and that we must face them."

"And for Caroline, who still believed in me and this story
after it lost to one about vampire shvantzes."

For more information, address:
Blue Boar Press
PO Box 204
Springvale, Maine 04083

Cover and Illustrations
Kate Whitmore

ISBN: 978-1-951478-00-1 (paperback)
ISBN: 978-1-951478-01-8 (ebook)

www.JasonHAbbott.com
www.BlueBoarPress.com

Additional Credits & Thanks

Manuscript Evaluation and Developmental Editing
by Lauren L. Garcia

Beta Reader Team:
Meiling Colorado
P. I. O'Neill
L. C. Priestley
Hannah Pryor
Charles Snow

And a special thank you to the
r/FantasyWriters community of authors on Reddit,
for the many years of critique and support they have
given me and countless others.

Jason H. Abbott

Emily's iPhone chimed and she checked it, the glitter of its pink case sparkling under the streetlight.

"She's just running late, angel," she texted in response. "Something with her cat. Still coming."

The sound of bicycle tires approaching in the night pulled her gaze off the screen, and to the paved road. She watched looping wheel reflectors glide out of the darkness.

"Hey, Em!" a boy in his teens huffed, peddling up the hill.

Seeing his chubby legs in cargo pants and Chuck Taylor high-tops struggling to crest the incline, Emily gave an eye-roll before he came to a stop beside her.

"Hi Sam," she said, looking back to her phone on the suburban curbside.

Emily quietly checked her Snapchat as he wheezed.

"You alright?" she asked.

"Yeah, I'm good," he answered, red, winded, and gulping cool autumn air. "Are you? I mean, with everything that's happened—"

"I'm just waiting for a ride," Emily said, confirming she still had Sam blocked on Snapchat. "I've only been here a few minutes."

Sam nodded, straightening the backpack on his shoulders. Within it clunked the binoculars he'd used to watch her for thirty minutes before riding up.

"Okay. Would you like me to stay until your ride gets here?"

The petite girl looked up from her iPhone. Her red skirt and cardigan were a new outfit, one not catalogued in the weeks of pictures and video Sam had taken of the cheerleader on his own phone now recording their conversation in his pocket.

Emily ran fingers through her blonde hair. "I—"

The lights of a car turning the corner illuminated the pair on the sidewalk.

"I'm good!" she finished. "My ride's here!"

A mauve '95 Dodge Neon came to a rattling stop alongside Emily. In the beams of its headlights, Sam squinted to see inside the old car now idling beside the curb.

Its teenage driver with bangs and long, straight hair met his gaze.

"Is that the new girl?" Sam asked.

"Yeah," Emily said, opening the front passenger door. "Melissa."

Melissa pushed up her thick framed glasses, giving him a small wave from behind the wheel.

"She's got a driver's license?" Sam asked.

Emily slipped into the car. "Uh-huh."

He pulled his bike onto the sidewalk. "Oh, okay. See you Monday?"

Emily slammed the door, then she grinned whispering to Melissa. "*Hopefully not.* Can we go please?"

The old beater shifted into gear, its dark-haired driver giving Sam a last look while both girls in the car exchanged laughs that were seen, but not heard. He returned Melissa's wave hesitantly, seeing her flash a smile in response before driving off.

The vehicle had barely reached the next streetlight before Sam opened his cargo pants pockets with the tear of Velcro. Quickly removing sticky patches of black electrical tape he'd prepped earlier, he slapped them over the headlight and reflectors of his bike.

"Goddammed parallel parking test," Sam grumbled, pulling back onto the street. Then he took off after the vehicle. "How the hell am I going to keep up with a car?!"

Furious peddling began, the phone in his pocket bouncing and recording squeaky wheels and renewed heavy breathing. Jostled, its sweaty touchscreen flicked on. The motion of his cycling swiped it into a video playback.

Of freshman Angie Brewer's headless corpse.

Digital glimpses of a blood-stained shed, and a splattered trail down the stairs of an abandoned basement.

Sam snarled with a hunter's determination; his eyes locked on the red taillights of Melissa's car.

Melissa glanced at Emily in the passenger seat. "Thanks again for inviting me."

Emily tuned and smiled; face illumed in the dark by the light of her phone. "You're welcome, it's fun to finally have our first hang out."

"Sorry I was late," Melissa nodded behind the wheel. "Dad was chatty, and dinner went long even before the whole thing with the cat."

"We haven't missed anything," Emily said. "I've been texting Roy."

"Great, I can't wait to meet everybody, and make some more friends. I'm kinda getting worried that I'll be *that new girl* forever, you know?"

"It's not you, it's just the shitty timing with everything that's happened," Emily said before her phone made a tinkling chime that drew her gaze. "Did you still have to lie to your dad to get out tonight?"

Frowning, Melissa nodded and tugged the shoulder of the too-large brown motorcycle jacket she wore. "Yeah. I didn't like it, but it wasn't hard to do on a Shabbat night. Dad just started his Torah study early."

"Are you breaking a commandment or something going to a little party?" Emily asked.

"No," Melissa chuckled. "At least, I don't think so. Religion's Dad's thing. I love him, but I only do it to make him happy."

Emily swiped her screen and smiled seeing a new text from Roy. "I get it. So what are we *officially* doing tonight, so we can get our stories straight?"

"We're watching movies at your house," Melissa said, sitting a little taller with a waggle of her shoulders.

"That sounds good," Emily said, gaze transfixed on the phone. "I haven't watched a movie in forever! Roy keeps me so busy, and he isn't into Netflix and chill."

Melissa's eyebrows rose behind her glasses before she cast a questioning look at Emily. "Well, I did bring my Hammer horror films collection along to make things look legit for Dad. Maybe we can watch one later? Or for our second hangout?"

"I've never heard of those," Emily said without looking up.

Melissa's eyes returned to the road as she slouched and sighed. *"Nobody has..."*

Emily continued to fiddle with her phone in silence, until Melissa began to rap her fingers in time to the car's rattling old engine on the steering wheel a minute later.

"Sooooooo," Melissa finally intoned. "Who was *that* guy back there?"

"Some boy from school," she answered, typing a text.

"Yeah, I've seen him around. He's kinda cute."

Emily snorted as she sent her message. "You need better glasses!"

"Nah, I like the shy ones! Is he your friend?"

"Sam? No!"

"Is he like a stalker creep or something?"

"No," Emily said, smiling at a thumbs-up emoji from Roy. "Not like that. He was just riding by and wanted to know if I was alright."

Melissa grinned making a turn. "Well, that's sweet! With Erin Bryer missing—"

"Angie," Emily interrupted flatly. "Her name was Angie. Angie Brewer."

"Sorry," Melissa apologized, raising an eyebrow. "She disappeared the week before I got here."

Emily gazed blankly through the windshield. "It's okay, you didn't know her. But that's her name."

Melissa tilted a glance at her friend's fixed-forward stare. "It, uh, wasn't the kind of thing my dad expected to happen here after moving us from the city. Did you know her?"

Emily turned to her. "Not well, but she was the sweetest thing. It makes me mad to think Sam could use whatever happened to her as an excuse to hit on me."

"That would be shitty," Melissa said, "but you don't know if that's true, do you?"

Her phone slumped in her grip. "You're right, I don't. It's all just so awful... We were going to hang-out the night she disappeared. I keep wondering if I'd showed up earlier, if maybe..."

Emily shook her head. "I don't want to think about it. It gives me nightmares."

The car fell silent again aside from its rattles as they accelerated onto a rural road.

"Maybe she ran away or something," Melissa said after a moment. "I don't know. Her parents are getting divorced, right?"

"Yeah."

"I can tell you how much that sucks. Maybe she's hiding somewhere, like with family in another state."

"Maybe."

"Anyways, this Sam guy: Does he have a girlfriend?"

"No," Emily chuckled.

"I wonder if he plays Magic the Gathering, or likes monster movies," Melissa pondered. "He seems like the type that would like old monster movies."

"No clue."

"Think he likes you?" Melissa asked.

"I always attract the weird ones. So, *probably.*"

"You say that like it's a bad thing."

"It's my curse."

"Weird can be fun, Em. I've been called weird. Weird means somebody's got depth that you can sink your teeth into, you know?"

Emily slid her iPhone into a matching pink purse. "Maybe? But I've got a wonderful boyfriend now. And I hope for Sam's sake he really isn't interested, because Roy's the jealous type."

"You're cool with that? I can't stand possessive guys."

"Oh, it's superficial. It'd be different if we went to the same school. Roy's an angel underneath it all."

"I'll take your word for it."

"It's the same with his temper," Emily said, smiling dreamily out the window.

Melissa furrowed her brow as they passed the *Welcome to Summersvale* sign. "Sounds like you're really into him."

"I am. He's one of those people that you just have to get to know a little before you realize how cool he is."

"Maybe Sam's the same way."

Emily giggled, turning from the window. "No, he's not like Roy."

"You don't know. Maybe Sam's a fun guy to see a movie with or—"

Emily burst out laughing, and Melissa winced at the sharp guffaws. "Are you serious?! One date with Sam Sherman and the whole school will be talking about it!"

Passing houses gave way to night-shrouded fields and trees as Melissa turned down a side road. "Maybe I am serious."

The blonde's bemused smirk subsided in rolling shadows. "Please tell me you're kidding?"

Melissa turned on the high beams tossing a grin at her friend. "Maybe I'm just weirder than you!"

"I'd say," Emily replied, blinking. "Whatever. Don't say I didn't warn you."

"*I won't*. Are we close to the fire pit?"

"The turn's coming right up."

"This isn't a thing with a ton of drugs or drinking, is it?"

"There might be a few beers?"

"Nobody's going to be sneaking into the woods and having sex, right?"

"Melissa!"

"I know! But—"

"It's a campfire!" Emily said, raising her hands. "Not an orgy!"

"Alright! Okay! But my dad only just let me have the keys back from the last time I was grounded and—"

Emily started tapping on the passenger window. "Pull in right here!"

Melissa's hiking shoe hit the brake, and the car lurched with a vibrating groan. Bracing herself at the noise, Emily looked at the pained smile Melissa flashed.

Squeaking and rattling, the jalopy, far older than its occupants, made the turn and entered the weedy dirt road. A slow series of bumps jostled the girls before they came to a stop a minute later in a gravel-strewn clearing.

Melissa looked about, the idling car's lights illuminating nothing but pine trees as far as they could see. "Nobody else is here."

"Maybe we're the first?" Emily replied, pulling out her phone again.

Melissa turned the keys, and the engine fell silent with a patter. "How late is this going to go if it hasn't even started yet?"

"Roy said he'd be here with the others."

"Unless there's another place to park you didn't tell me about, he isn't."

Emily tapped out and sent a text in seconds. "Maybe it got called off?"

"Weren't you texting him when I picked you up?" Melissa asked.

Emily unbuckled her seatbelt. "Yeah, and I'm going to be pissed if he's playing games and I dragged you out here for nothing!"

"Well, if it isn't happening," Melissa said, leaning in, "we *could* drive back to your house and watch—"

The door opened with a rusty squeal.

"Hey, where are you going?" Melissa asked.

"Even if we've been stood-up or pranked, I'm at *least* going to show you the stars out here!" Emily answered. "They're beautiful when it's clear like this."

"Awesome," Melissa mumbled, switching off the headlights and pulling the keys from the ignition. "Next time I'm trying my luck with bicycle boy."

Stepping from the car into the growing chill of a cloudless night, she shivered and glanced at Emily, who wore only her skirt and cardigan.

"Aren't you cold?" Melissa asked, her breath a cloud of mist. "Didn't you bring a coat?"

"My love for Roy keeps me warm," she answered, smiling with her gaze fixed upwards.

Melissa rolled her eyes unseen, then began closing buttons on her oversized jacket. "Well, I'm freezing. I'm glad Dad let me borrow his biker jacket after I found the cat had barfed on my hoodie!"

"Gross."

"Yeah, it was fleece too. Warmer than this thing."

"Come see this," Emily said. "We have a wonderful view of *Draco* right now."

Melissa cracked a mischievous grin behind her. "Is he, *fighting Harry Potter?*"

"No. He's next to *Ursa Minor.*"

Shaking her head amused, Melissa jangled the keys dangling off the little cylinder she held. Emily spoke again as her friend's thumb found the worn fob button and locked the car.

"There's a trail through the woods that'll take us to where they'll light the fire, if there is one. It goes past the Clapson graveyard."

Sliding her keys and both hands into the pockets of the jacket, Melissa tucked her fingers against the warmth of her waist. "A graveyard. At night. In October?"

"You should see it," Emily said, still looking up. "I've only been there during the day, I bet it's real creepy at night!"

Melissa felt the pointed edges of the steel charm hanging off the tip of the key cylinder. Joining her friend in looking up at the stars, her finger traced the outline of the six-pointed star in her pocket. "I don't know, sounds like the start of every bad horror movie I've ever seen to me."

"But I thought you *liked* horror movies? You said so."

"Yeah, I like to watch them. Not *be* in them."

As she finished speaking, puzzlement washed over Melissa's face as she found a small bundle beside her keys in the pocket.

"Well, suit yourself," Emily continued. "I'm going to—"

"*Oh, Dad!*" Melissa half-groaned, half-shouted looking at the black cubes she'd pulled from her father's jacket.

Startled, Emily spun around and faced her. "What?!"

The dark-haired girl stood shaking her head at her palm, looking at a pair of small boxes neatly wrapped in the leather strap that joined them.

"What's that?" Emily asked.

"It's my Dad's," Melissa said. "It's a prayer thing, and important to him. I just can't believe the stuff he'll forget in his pockets sometimes! This shouldn't even be in a pocket!"

"Uh, alright?" Emily said, now with her own puzzled look.

She stuffed the *tefillin* back in the jacket. "You should see the stuff I find when it's my turn to do laundry!"

The girls shared a laugh as Melissa walked across crunching gravel.

A head shorter than her friend, Emily turned and resumed pointing out the constellations above. "Like I was saying, the stars are beautiful out here. No lights from town to spoil them. We've got *Draco* there, and *Ursa Minor* trying to bite him. And of course, there's Polaris right at the tip of *Ursa's* tail."

Melissa smiled, looking up. "You know what I said about liking weird people, because they have depth?"

"Yeah?"

"You have *depth*."

Emily scrunched her face.

"You hang-out in graveyards. You talk like an astronomer. You, Em, are *weird*."

"Please, don't tell anyone," Emily requested.

Melissa looked to the pine treetops, and pushed up her glasses above a grin. "Sure."

The ring of cellphone startled them both.

"Is that Roy?" Melissa asked, semi-snickering after the scare.

A second ring came, and Melissa's expression became concerned as she turned to Emily and discovered the noise wasn't coming from her purse.

Patting the phone in her pocket and finding it still and silent, Melissa heard the ring a third time.

Coming up behind her.

"Ah crap," a rough, masculine voice cursed.

Emily looked past her with a blissful grin. "Roy!"

Before Melissa could turn, a pair of hands slammed down on her sides and yanked her backwards. With a putrid smell, a throaty hiss passed her ear.

She screamed, kicked, and struggled immediately. Slipping partially free thanks to her oversized jacket, the snap of biting teeth missed Melissa's neck.

"Let me go!" she yelled. "Em', help!"

Swung like a toy in a vice grip, her panicked thrashing and sliding within the loose jacket landed an elbow in the side of her unseen attacker. The adrenaline-fueled blow sent a wave of pain through her arm as it struck corpulent flesh and ribs, but only evoked a foul-smelling grunt from them.

"Hold her!" the gratingly rough voice behind her commanded.

Melissa remained grappled but struggling as Emily nodded with euphoric calm.

"What are you doing?!" Melissa shouted.

"Please don't fight," Emily said, reaching for her. "Roy wants to make you a beautiful angel. Like him."

Melissa thwapped a hard kick into Emily's stomach, and the lithe teen was knocked onto her back.

"What the fuck is this?! You're crazy!"

"It's scary, I'm sorry," Emily wheezed on the ground. "But he's giving you the gift of eternal life. Someday, Roy will share it with me, too!"

Roy's voice creaked like an old door. "Get up and grab her legs, Puppet!"

"I'm sorry," Emily replied dragging herself up. "So sorry. I'm weird. Please don't tell anybody..."

Melissa saw her enthralled eyes and smile, then lashed out anew against Roy's iron grip.

He swung her hard to the right, whipping Melissa's head and sending her glasses sailing into the darkness amid flailing hair. Vision now a blur, she saw Emily rush forward. With her free arm still throbbing from the blow she'd landed on Roy's side, Melissa reached into her pocket.

Her hand withdrew clenching the grey cylinder on her keyring. Popping off its cap, she squeezed a faceful of pepper spray into Emily's tranquil eyes and smile.

An agonized wail followed as Emily keeled over, blinded and writhing.

"Damn you!" Roy growled. "Now I'll have to break and *spoil* you!"

Emily cried and rolled on the gravel while Roy hoisted Melissa aloft like a child. The grip on her shoulders increased to a crushing pain as she caught sight of Roy's ruddy, bloated hand upon her. His ragged fingernails punctured her father's leather jacket, and unable to aim the pepper spray, Melissa instead gripped the steel charm amongst her keys and thrust the star into Roy's arm.

Its pointed edge plunged deep into red, swollen flesh... and an inhuman bellow echoed through the trees.

Not released so much as thrown, Melissa's heels hit the ground and she scrambled to remain standing. After almost tripping over the still-screaming Emily, she faced her attacker.

He was monstrous and rancid: A bloated and balding figure under the starlight, ruddy skin stretched so tight that it split and tore in patches. Shirtless and barefoot, Roy wore only sweatpants as he clutched a hand emitting a dying wisp of acrid smoke amid a sound like hissing acid.

Melissa stepped back, lifting the trembling keys and pepper spray that were her only weapons.

"You," he said between heavy breaths that produced no mist in the cold air. Then he looked up from the wound and locked his gaze on her. *"You suck."*

"Who— *What* are you?" she yelled, thrusting the keychain at him.

He retreated a step, and Melissa blinked in surprise.

"Roy," Emily sobbed, clenched palms covering her face. "It hurts!"

His eyes— sunken, dark pools around red pinhole embers— didn't move from Melissa.

"What do you think I am?" he asked, then gnashed out a ravenous growl that displayed his fanged canines.

Melissa straightened a shaking arm and squeezed the pepper spray trigger. "I think you're stupid to stand still like a target!"

She hosed his face with pepper spray until the canister sputtered empty. But as the mist dispersed, he stood unaffected. Red eyes still fixed on her.

"Mmm. *Spicy,*" Roy mocked, residue dribbling off his chin.

"She's terrible!" Emily cried. "Roy, she doesn't deserve your gift like Angie did!"

Melissa looked at her rolling on the ground. "Angie? You—"

Hunched and watching her with predatory intensity, Roy attempted to lunge. But with a swipe of her keys, he lurched back and remained at bay.

"Why do you have that!?" he demanded over Emily's sobs.

The supernatural presence continued to glare at Melissa. Then she noticed the monster's gaze was not locked on her, so much as it was on her hand.

"How did you get something blessed by a priest!?" Roy yelled.

She gasped looking at the Star of David dangling from her keyring. "Holy shit!"

"Something like that," Roy rasped back.

"What are you?" Melissa asked, returning her eyes to the fiend. "A Jewish vampire?"

"No, there's just something about the pointless symbols of covenant from gods that have long since abandoned mankind," he smiled darkly.

Melissa took a step forward, and watched Roy recoil an equal distance. "It isn't pointless to my dad. And it doesn't seem *pointless* to you, either!"

Roy scowled. "A rabbi's daughter, huh? Great. *Mazel tov*. Puppet, you sure can pick 'em!"

Emily wept hearing his words. "I'm sorry, I didn't know before! I'm so sorry my angel..."

"Why not a nice, tasty atheist?" Roy continued. "But no, you bring me a stubborn girl from a stubborn faith too stupid to know God's abandoned them!"

"Hey!" Melissa shouted. "Shut up you, you... *Shvantz!*"

"Ooh," Roy taunted, leaning in. "Did I touch a nerve and bring out your Grammie's Yiddish?"

She thrust the star and he pulled back. "Fuck off!"

Roy's laugh was deep, like an untuned drum. "But it's true. Your god, *all* gods... they all gave up on you and mankind a *long* time ago." He pointed at the Star of David. "Where was God when I watched your people put in ovens? Nowhere. But the smell, oh now that was *divine!*"

"I, I don't believe you!" Melissa stammered.

"Neither did the last girl," Roy said. "She prayed to Christ as I put my teeth in her..."

He trailed off, running a blue-black tongue over yellowed canine fangs as if savoring a taste. "But the power of Christ didn't compel me to stop. Or stop her from *rising*. She even rose, *early*."

"Angel-Angie flew away on her wings," Emily whimpered.

"No," Roy groaned, "she got out of the shed Puppet didn't lock tight enough when we left!"

Curled into a ball, Emily pawed her face and cried.

"But we'll find her, Puppet," he continued, still fixated on Melissa. "And soon add another!"

"You're both crazy!" Melissa yelled.

Roy flashed a predatory smile. "Then run! Turn your back! You won't make it to the car!"

"I can pull an all-nighter standing here until dawn! Can you?"

He pursed his lips into a mocking pout. "Won't have to. Puppet will recover soon. She'll keep you and your trinket occupied for the moment I need to end this little standoff."

"Yes, Angel," Emily wept. "It just hurts so bad!"

Melissa did a quick double-take between Emily and Roy, then snarled and shouted wide-eyed at him. "Motherfucker! You've been playing me for time!"

Another roll of Roy's throaty laughter echoed off the pines.

Melissa whipped out her cell phone. "Are you going to laugh for the cops after I call 911?"

Roy stopped laughing, his face pinching and souring as Melissa gave a half-glance to the phone's touchscreen to place an emergency call. He crouched as she began to swipe, grasping a stone at his feet and slinging it with blinding speed and force. The rock hit the smartphone, and it cartwheeled into the dark from Melissa's hand with a completely shattered screen.

She thrust the Star of David between them, and Roy retreated a step with a raspy chuckle.

"I hope your carrier plan covers damage," he said, reaching down and grabbing a bigger rock.

He chucked the rock and it whizzed at Melissa's head. She barely ducked it, and a second later it knocked a splintered chunk out of a tree behind her.

Seeing the star lowered from her dodge, Roy bellowed and lunged.

Melissa countered with a split-second dash of her own. Kicking up dirt in a zig-zag feint, she outmaneuvered Roy. His tackle ending as a skidding belly-flop across gravel, Melissa darted past and for her car.

Her sprint ended with a bang against the side of the vehicle. A fumbling fob button press and quick grab opened the door. But as she scrambled in, Melissa's head snapped back, and she was yanked from salvation.

"No," Roy said, his hand gripping her long hair.

He grabbed the keys and threw them, attached holy symbol and all, into the woods. Then with a growling laugh, he lifted her above his head and slammed her back-first onto the car's hood.

Melissa curled up and gasped for air as ragged fingers clutched her throat.

"A good try," Roy hoarsely whispered into her ear. "But let me tell you something my puppet doesn't know before you die: There are no more angels, here or in heaven... there is only we who were despised. The discarded. We're all but stars in the night now. Lost. Waiting for the forever dark to come."

Licking cracked lips, he blew a putrid breath on her neck and watched Melissa struggle futilely in a grip as strong and cold as iron.

"You've made me hungry," he said. "I'll enjoy seeing your corpse rise."

Roy leaned in to bite, but stopped short as something rounded the turn from the weedy dirt road and came to a jerking halt in the clearing.

"Get the hell away from her!" Sam Sherman yelled.

Roy slowly turned his head, facing the teen with a fanged mixture of surprise and annoyance. "Seriously?"

"Get off her!" Sam shouted from astride his bike.

"Who the hell are you?" Roy snarled, still choking Melissa.

Sam pulled off his backpack. "Just some kid!"

Roy growled, thudding Melissa back onto the hood of the car. "Just some kid, huh?"

"Yeah," Sam said unzipping his pack.

Beginning a stalking advance, Roy dragged Melissa one-handed beside him. "You're going to be a *dead* kid in a moment!"

"Angel? What's happening?" Emily whimpered in the background.

"Dinner's just become a buffet, Puppet," Roy answered, quickening his pace.

Thrashing nearly breathless, Melissa landed a kick on Roy that evoked a glare upon her.

"Don't worry," Roy smirked, "You're still the main course: I prefer lean meat!"

"Let her go!" Sam yelled.

Roy looked back to him, ready to lunge. Then froze.

The teen leveled something akin to a pistol-gripped shotgun he'd withdrawn from his backpack. "I won't let you do to her what you did to Angie!"

"What?" Roy said, looking down the barrel pointed at him. "What did you say?"

"I found her body," Sam said, resolutely. "I hid it, and you were too stupid to figure out what really happened!"

"Where's my scion, boy?" Roy snarled. "Tell me where my newly risen is! Or I'll—"

Roy stopped mid-sentence, squinting. Then a slow, rattling laugh began to build until he bellowed out a guffaw.

The weapon Sam held in the dark was a water gun spray-painted black.

"You've got balls to bluff like that, boy!" Roy shouted. "And now, I'm going to rip them off."

Sam pulled back on the pump as Roy rushed forward. "Who's bluffing?!"

Not attempting to dodge, the gush of fluid drenched Roy's face. It splattered on Melissa in his grip, and the grey liquid assaulted her senses with the pungent smell of concentrated garlic mixed with a metallic odor.

Soaked by the concoction now draining onto his sweatpants, Roy's grip tightened on Melissa's neck. Fighting against unconsciousness, she saw the liquid begin to smoke and bubble on his rancid hand.

A bestial wail pierced the night, and Melissa hit the ground free of Roy's grapple.

"Angel! Oh, my angel!" Emily screamed.

Sam threw the emptied gun aside and reached anew into his pack. "You like it? Garlic juice, powdered silver, and holy water… I made a homebrew!"

Melissa sat up, wiping the mixture off her brow and choking down breaths while Roy staggered, blundered and finally fell, loosing a howl of utter agony. Rolling plumes of acrid smoke drifted off him, dimming starlight and making a sizzling sound like cooking bacon between his screams.

"I didn't know what folklore was bullshit, and what would work," Sam said, unsheathing a machete he'd removed from the backpack. "So I covered all the bases, and I guess you don't like any of them!"

Emily screamed, writhing as Sam charged incapacitated Roy. "I can feel his pain! Stop hurting my angel!"

Reaching the monster as he smoked and beat the ground in blind agony, Sam paid her no heed lifting the machete to cleave Roy's neck.

"This is for Angie, you son of a bitch!" he shouted, swiping the blade down.

Roy seized Sam's arm with the supernatural speed and strength within his swollen limbs. The blow stopped dead, Sam felt his sneakers and all two hundred and thirty pounds of him leave the ground as Roy rose.

Bloated flesh boiled and burned away to reveal patches of teeth and skull, Roy continued to sizzle while he grabbed the young man's throat.

Sam struggled as Roy moved to snap his neck. But a leather loop dropped past Roy's face, and in a pause of shock he looked down as it fell around his neck.

Holding the ends of the tefillin in both hands, Melissa placed a foot on his back and pulled her father's phylactery taut.

Roy dropped Sam on his backside. Reeling and stumbling away from him, Roy's ragged nails clawed the prayer object that smoked and burned across his neck. Fighting to maintain the garrote, monstrous strength swung Melissa wildly left and right as Sam leapt up, abandoning his blade.

"Stop it!" Emily screamed as Roy's neck flared with fire. "I can feel my Angel dying!"

Sam grabbed the tefillin's leather straps. His eyes wide with the same terror that filled Melissa's, the pair's gaze met as he yelled. "Don't stop!"

His cry a rally, they leaned into an all-out pull.

Roy shoved his fingers into his blazing flesh, prying at the strap with all his might and desperation. His frenzy began to overcome the teen's combined strength as they slowly lost the tug-of-war.

Then Roy's arms slapped forward, loosing his grip while Sam and Melissa regained theirs. Feeling Roy's resistance ebb, the pair united and heaved on the straps. Roy's bare feet dragged past his now severed, burning fingers on the ground.

Emily released a tortured, ear-splitting scream. Melissa winced at the sound, but her hand remained anchored beside Sam's above the tefillin's cubes... and the Torah passages contained within them.

The leather slid a little longer. There was a snap, and then Sam and Melissa banged against the car.

Emily collapsed, silent. In the sudden absence of her hysteria, something hit the ground and rolled.

Holding the strap between them, Sam and Melissa watched Roy's body stumble forward. Fingerless palms passing through smoke above headless shoulders, it fell over.

The teens slid down the side of the car to the ground. There they stared at the aftermath for a long minute, quick breaths misting in cold air.

"Did we," Melissa finally asked. "Did we just kill a fucking vampire?"

Sam gulped. "Yeah. I think so."

She turned narrowed eyes to him. "How did you know?"

"I've been following Emily for weeks," he replied, "trying to find him."

"You just let her lead me into a trap?" Melissa said, giving him a shove. "What the hell!"

"Em's popular!" He shoved back. "She sees lots of people! I'm sorry, but I didn't know if she was bringing you to the bloodsucker, or if you two were really just hanging out!"

Sam looked away, crossing arms and resting them on folded knees. "I could only find him if they didn't know I was looking. I couldn't mess up. Not even once. And I couldn't do or say anything that might have tipped them off unless I was absolutely certain!"

Melissa watched him brood, and her hard glare faded as she touched his shoulder. "I'm sorry, I didn't think about it like that."

"It's alright," he said, glancing at her touch. "It's crazy. Maybe what I did was crazy. Maybe that's just what happens when you find out monsters are real."

"You're not crazy," Melissa said. "How'd you learn about all this?"

He rubbed his thick neck, then pointed to a dark path going uphill through the trees at the end of the clearing.

"I was recording in the old Clapson Graveyard. I had this idea about making something creepy and putting it up on YouTube. Anyways, I found a lost composition book up there beside a tombstone. The first half was notes and homework, but the second half read like a weird cross between a movie script and a love letter."

"Em's?" Melissa asked.

Sam nodded. "She hadn't written her name on it. I had to flip through a lot to figure out it was hers."

He looked at Melissa. "The stuff in the back read like fiction. It got weird mentioning Angie

Brewer and other girls from school, but I thought it was a draft of a script, or some Halloween thing she was doing with friends. I almost gave it back to her the next day, but then Angie disappeared."

His gaze wandered to the shadowed trees. "That's when I followed the notes and found Angie's body in the shed, right where the notebook said they would stash it."

"Why didn't you call the cops?" Melissa asked.

Sam's eyes returned to hers, dead serious. "Because Angie rose when I found her. *Hungry.*"

"Oh God..."

"It's not like *Twilight*, or *Interview with the Vampire*," he continued. "You don't come back to life as a vampire: *You don't come back at all*. They never were people. They're something, else."

Melissa shook her head. "I don't understand."

"It's like possession, except instead of a living person they take over a corpse."

"They don't have bodies? Like ghosts?"

"You've got the idea, but most lore calls them *demons*," Sam said. "They're ancient, and evil. And if you don't kill them the right way, they'll just keep coming back in other bodies."

Sam grabbed the side of the car and pulled himself to his feet. "Whatever was in Angie came after me like a rabid animal."

He lifted the bottom of his shirt, and Melissa flinched at the raked cuts and claw marks across his stomach.

"She almost got me," he said, covering his healing wounds. "But I got ahold of a shovel in the shed."

"You fought her off?"

Sam nodded as Melissa stood. "I slapped her off with it, but she was relentless. Finally, I knocked her down, got the spade under her chin…"

Falling silent, he made a motion as if holding a downward pointed shovel. Then lifting a foot onto an imaginary spade, his heel thudded the ground as his hands conveyed a deep thrust.

"And that's why you didn't call the cops," Melissa said.

He met her eyes. "I didn't think that would end well for me."

"I don't know," she shrugged, "Maybe you could've been like: *Yes, that's right officer. The varsity cheerleading captain is working with a vampire and he's the one that killed the missing freshman.*"

"*I'll even take you to where I hid Angie's body, Mr. Cop,*" Sam added to the air of gallows humor.

"Just remember that I had to mutilate her corpse after she rose as an undead."

Melissa folded hands to her shoulders against a chill. "So, then you learned everything you could about vampires, to stop them yourself."

"Pretty much. I found some old books, and a couple things that might be true from the crazy conspiracy side of the internet."

She offered a handshake. "You saved my ass. I'm glad you went full *Van Helsing.*"

"I don't know," Sam said, accepting her grip. "What you did with that tefillin was brilliant and badass. I would've never thought of that!"

Melissa held up the phylactery. "It's my dad's. The Star of David on my keys hurt Roy and kept him back, so I figured he really wouldn't like this."

"Just like the holy water I hit him with in the mix," he half-smirked as they continued to shake hands. "That stuff wasn't easy to get, but I guess it was worth it."

"How do you even know what a tefillin is?"

"Your dad's Kadelburg, right? The new rabbi at Beth? With the *Harley?*"

"Yeah. But—"

"*Samuel Sherman*, nice to meet you," he said. "I had my *bar mitzvah* at *Temple Beth.*"

"Oh," she replied before thinking about it an additional second. Then she began to shake his hand more vigorously. "Oh! *Shalom alechem!*"

"*Alechem shalom,*" he grinned as their hands remained clasped. "And when you call me *Van Helsing*, are you talking Hugh Jackman, or Peter Cushing? 'Cause that's important."

Melissa answered his budding smile with her own. "I *thought* you'd be into old monster movies! Cushing. It's definitely Cushing."

Emily stirred from her place on the ground, then released a whimper drawing their attention.

"Is she one of them?" Melissa asked, releasing Sam's hand.

He took a step towards Emily and motioned her to follow. "No."

"Help me," Emily muttered weakly. "Somebody help me..."

"He was controlling her," Sam said as they reached her. "Roy made her his thrall."

Melissa crouched and touched her. "His what?"

"His *Renfield*. You know, like in *Dracula?* Like *enthralled*. He was controlling her mind."

"Mel?" Emily asked. "Are you okay?"

Melissa held her hand. "Yeah."

Emily tried to rise. "Is it over? Is Roy gone? It feels like waking up."

"It's over," Sam said. Then he glanced at Roy's severed head and still smoking neck. "*Almost.*"

"Sam?" Emily asked.

He kneeled beside her and Melissa. "Uh-huh, I'm good."

"You found my book?"

Sam and Melissa exchanged glances before helping her to sit upright.

"It's like waking up," Emily reiterated, hoarse from screaming. "From a nightmare. From doing horrible things that made so much sense until..."

Emily covered a face streaked with tears from irritant and raw emotion, then wailed.

"I held Angie down as he hurt her!" she sobbed as Melissa clutched Emily.

Sam gripped Emily's shoulder as she bawled, his lips on the verge of speaking, but unable to do so.

"Sometimes," she choked between tears, "It was almost like waking up. Like a dream inside a dream. I could see how wrong it was!"

Emily glared at the stars, then raise a fist clenched so tight that her manicured nails drew blood from her palms. "But he always pushed me back down!"

She slumped languid as Melissa rocked and consoled her. "Not your fault, Em."

"I smiled helping him kill poor Angie," Emily sniffed. "I almost did the same to you..."

"You tried to fight it," Melissa said. "Did you know Sam had your notebook?"

"It was one of those moments," Emily answered weakly. "I'd seen Roy, in the graveyard. I saw Sam after, and hid. I knew I only had a thought or two before Roy would push me back down, back into the nightmare... so I tried to yell, knowing he'd sense and stop me."

Emily looked at Sam and tried to smile. "I don't believe in God, but as Roy pushed me down, I prayed he wouldn't know I also dropped the notebook."

She buried her face in Melissa's jacket and embrace as Melissa looked at Sam, crying her own tears.

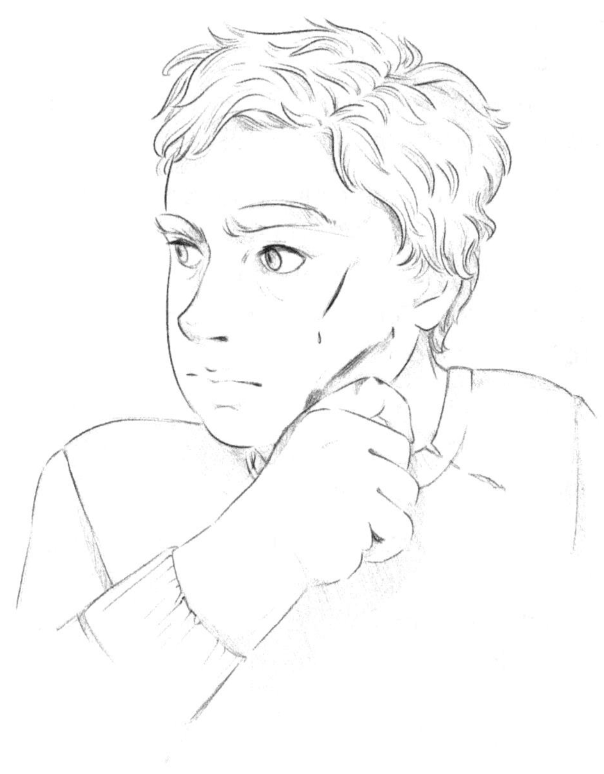

"Right there," Emily said, pointing to a small and decrepit mausoleum. She tightened a blanket from the car over her cardigan before Melissa and Sam passed her dragging Roy's headless body by his bare ankles.

"That's where he caught me," she continued. "I could only hear him. He was calling for help, saying he was a hiker that had fallen in exploring the graveyard. Then I saw him, and it was too late."

Sam watched Emily dab her eyes on a shirtsleeve. "Well, now he's going in there for good."

"This guy weighs a fucking ton!" Melissa strained as the pair pulled the bloated body through the doorway. "You sure nobody's going to find him and call the cops?"

"He'll rot to bones in a few days," he grunted in the cramped interior. "And be dust in weeks. That's what happened to Angie's body, anyway."

Emily's hand was unsteady shining her iPhone from the entrance, but the shaky light was enough for them to see. With a final tug, the teens hauled the corpse to the rear of the mausoleum and dropped Roy's legs with a thud.

Something fell out of Roy's sweatpants, clattering to a stop beside Sam's Chuck Taylors and a mortar-sealed floor crypt.

"What's that?" Melissa asked as Sam crouched down.

He lifted a Samsung. "A, phone?"

"Oh yeah, I'd forgotten," Melissa said as he turned it on. "He got a call, and that's why he didn't get the total drop on me."

"He'd text me all the time," Emily groaned in the doorway. "I don't think he was ever off it!"

"Dumbass never set a screen lock," Sam muttered, turning it on.

Melissa peered over his shoulder, squinting past a chip in her recovered glasses. "What's on it?"

"Emails and Facebook," he said, flipping through screens with finger swipes. "Oh my God, and there's some group called Vlad and I don't like the look of it at all!"

Then he paused after a final swipe.

"Is that, Pokémon GO?" Melissa said, pointing.

The trio exchanged perplexed glances.

Sam turned off the phone. "We'll have to check this out later, but we need to take care of the rest now."

They pulled the rusty mausoleum door shut, then walked in silence past mossy tombstones in the old Clapson Graveyard. The October night had grown more crisp and chill under the stars, and exiting the semi-straight path between the graves they looked down the hill to the graveled clearing. Melissa's Dodge Neon and Sam's bicycle remained alone.

Sam picked up his backpack that leaned on a tree.

"It's up this path," Emily said with a shiver.

A five-minute walk along the woods and tall field grass brought them to a simple stone fire ring, and a log to sit on.

The girls watched Sam place the backpack on the ground, then unzip the top.

"Is he still aware?" Melissa asked.

Sam looked down. "Yeah, but he can't do much about anything."

Emily nodded. "I can, *feel* him in there. Somehow."

"I've read that former thralls sometimes gain a kind of sixth-sense about vampires," Sam said, carefully reaching into the pack. "You might be one of those now."

"A power," Melissa said, "Em, you're a psychic!"

"But I don't want to be *weirder!*"

"You don't have to fight it, if you embrace it," her friend smiled back.

Emily shook her head and sighed before turning back to Sam. "But they'll still never be able to control me again, like you said?"

He lifted Roy's head from the backpack. "Never. Everything I've found makes it sound like being an ex-thrall makes you immune."

The head snapped and gnashed fangs, and Sam warily held it at a distance as they stepped beside the stone ring.

"Watch your fingers," Melissa said.

"Yeah, he's mad," Emily added. "And, scared."

Melissa squatted as Roy's head was placed at the center of the stones. She then picked-up a clump of dirt. "Can he hear and see us?"

"I guess," Sam said, moving to grab dry wood nearby.

She watched Roy's ember-red eyes give her an angry sideways glare.

Melissa responded by hitting Roy with a faceful of tossed dirt. "Good."

Sam leaned some sticks against Roy's skull. "I've got a newspaper and lighter fluid in my pack, can somebody get that?"

Melissa got up. "On it."

"Why fire?" Emily asked, looking down at Roy.

"If you just destroy the body, the spirit will eventually enter another corpse and return,"

Sam answered. "But it's said in lore that if you burn the head within three days, you consign them to flame forever."

Melissa returned with crumpled newsprint. Together, they stuffed it around Roy like a collar. His expression grew ever more fearful as Sam uncapped the lighter fluid and squirted its entire contents over him.

With the container empty, he looked to Melissa. "Did you grab the matches too?"

She lifted a cardboard box of kitchen matches. "Yeah, but..."

Sam tilted his head at her trailing pause. "But what?"

"We just beat this... this *putz*, with *religion*," Melissa said glaring at Roy. "But now we're two Jews about to kindle a fire on the *Shabbat*."

"Oh man," Sam said smacking his head. "I hadn't even *thought* about that!"

"Is it bad to do this breaking a *melakhah?*" she asked.

"I don't know," Sam shrugged. "You're the rabbi's daughter!"

"Do you want me to *call* him?" Melissa asked, squinting over her glasses. *"Hey Dad. Hypothetically, does pikuach nefesh cover lighting a fire to burn a vampire's head on Shabbat?"*

"I can do it," Emily said faintly behind them.

"I just don't know, Mel," Sam said scratching his head. "I'm pretty sure it covers everything else we've done tonight, and I don't even know if will matter... but we really don't want to screw this up!"

"I'll do it!" Emily said, forcefully enough to turn her friends' attention to her. "I don't know what you're talking about, but I'm not Jewish. I can do it."

Melissa shook her head. "Em, honey, no. You've been through enough!"

Emily's nod was weak, but sure. "I'll do it, for *Angie*."

"You don't have to," Sam said, reaching to take the matches. "I'll—"

Emily snatched the box from Melissa with a shaking hand before he could. "I *want* to do it."

Sam and Melissa stepped aside, and Emily knelt beside the fire ring. Her gaze met the most pleading expression Roy's gruesome visage could muster.

She struck the match against the box, then held it in front of his eyes.

Her tears reflected its flickering light. "You filled my mind with angels. With love and light. But it was all lies, and illusions, and dreams... just to make me your *tool*."

Emily smelled the mix of sulfur from the match, and butane from the fluid. "You didn't tell Mel there was no Heaven. So even if there is no God, I'm praying that you go to Hell!"

She flicked the match onto saturated newsprint, and a flash of flame engulfed Roy's head before Emily had finished standing. Taking only a lone step back, she watched the intensifying blaze for several minutes.

Striking more matches.

One by one.

Throwing them into the fire.

Until the box was empty.

No one spoke as she returned, walked past her friends, and sat on the log as the pyre crackled.

Melissa was the first to sit beside her. Then Sam joined them, finding Melissa's hand as he took a seat.

Emily gazed into flame. "He *made* me believe in angels."

Melissa looked at Sam, squeezing his fingers. "He told me, there were no angels."

"He was lying," Sam said.

"He *was*," Emily nodded. "I had two come to save me."

Embers drifted upwards, then faded to darkness between the stars.

About the Author

Jason H. Abbott is an author of fantasy, science fiction and more. Born a lobsterman's son in a small coastal town, he spent his youth exploring the woods and rocky beaches of Maine pursuing make-believe and adventures. These journeys eventually led him down many paths less traveled, and to a storyteller's life where the power of myths both ancient and modern are his inspirations.

An active indie and social media author, Jason shares daily original micro and flash fiction between working on longer projects. These include several ongoing microfiction series and miniseries', and numerous one-shot "very short stories" often no longer than a Twitter tweet. You can learn more about Jason, his available works, and follow him across many platforms by visiting his author's site at JasonHAbbott.com.